KU-239-857

Postman Pat's
Summer Storybook

by John Cunliffe
Illustrated by Celia Berridge
from the original Television designs by Ivor Wood

ANDRE DEUTSCH

First published in 1987 by
André Deutsch Limited
105–106 Great Russell Street London WC1B 3LJ

Text copyright © 1987 by John Cunliffe
Illustrations copyright © 1987 by Celia Berridge
and Woodland Animations Limited
All rights reserved

British Library Cataloguing in Publication Data

Cunliffe, John
   Postman Pat's summer story book.
   I. Title   II. Berridge, Celia
   823'.914[J]   PZ7

   ISBN 0-233-98078-4

Printed and bound by L.E.G.O, Vicenza, Italy

Contents

Pat and Jim

It was summer in Greendale, and a lovely sunny morning. There were two postmen in Pat's van, as it drove along the valley – Pat and Jim. Jess had to ride on Jim's knee. Mrs. Goggins smiled when she saw them coming to collect the day's letters.

"I see you have a helper today, Pat."

"Yes," said Pat. "This is Jim. I'm going on holiday next week, and Jim's going to deliver my letters whilst I'm away. I'm showing him the best way round, so he won't get lost."

"He'll be all right," said Mrs. Goggins, "if it keeps fine."

"It'll be as good as a holiday to me," said Jim. "It's a grand place is Greendale."

Pat showed Mrs. Goggins his holiday brochures. "Have a look at this," he said. "Brighton!"

"Brighton," she said. "Doesn't it look nice. Sea and sun, and no letters. I went there with Auntie Nellie when I was six."

"We'd better be on our way with these letters," said Pat.

"Make sure he doesn't leave any gates open," said Mrs. Goggins.

"Righto!" said Pat. "Cheerio!"

Pat and Jim were on their way.

Everyone was surprised to see two postmen coming with the letters, and Pat had to stop to tell them all about his holiday. It took twice as long as usual to get round. At Greendale Farm, when they heard that Pat was going to Brighton, Katy and Tom ran to rummage in their toy cupboard. Tom brought Pat a spade, and Katy brought a bright yellow bucket.

"So you can build a beautiful big sand-castle," she said.

"And you must take a camera," said Mrs. Pottage, rumpling about in a drawer. "I know I have one here somewhere. I never use it. You'll be able to show us the pictures when you come back. Here it is, and it even has a film in it."

"Well, that's very kind of you all. Thank you very much," said Pat. "We'd better be on our way, now, or I'll never get to Brighton. Cheerio!"

Off went Pat and Jim, along the wandering Greendale roads.

"Next stop, Thompson Ground," said Pat. "Now if you take this back road, you'll be there in half the time."

And so they were. Mrs. Thompson was all agog to hear about Pat's holiday.

"Brighton?" she said. "Fancy, going all that way; but they say it's lovely in the sea. You'll have to go for a swim at Brighton. Now there's a lovely bathing costume and a pair of water-wings in the wardrobe, and Alf has never worn them. Do take them."

Off she went, and soon came back with an old-fashioned costume, in red and green stripes, and a huge set of floats. They gave Jess a fright when Pat put them in the van.

Away went Pat and Jim, up and over the hills, and round twisting and twining corners.

"Watch out for this next bend," said Pat, "it's a bad one."

"Ooops!" said Jim. "You're not joking."

Jess hung on with all his claws. He knew that bend well.

They were soon at Ted Glen's workshop. He was busy mending Granny Dryden's television.

"Am I seeing double?" said Ted. "That's what comes of mending your own glasses."

"No, there are two of us," said Pat. "This is Jim." He told Ted all about his holiday in Brighton.

"Well," said Ted, "if you're going down South you'll be able to do some walking on the Sussex Downs. You can borrow my rucksack, it's under here somewhere."

Ted began to dig about under a jumble of old papers and magazines behind Mrs. Thompson's grandfather clock, that had been waiting at least five years to be mended. He found a pair of brown shoes, a cushion, and a wizened apple.

"I've been looking everywhere for those shoes," said Ted.

Then he found the rucksack. It was very dusty, and it made them sneeze when he shook it.

"There we are. Grand!" said Ted. "Oh, there's an old sandwich in it. Now I wonder how long that's been there?"

It was covered in green mould. "A long time," said Pat, "by the look of it."

Ted dropped the sandwich in the stove. "You'll be all right with this," he said. "You'll have a great time. Cheerio!"

There was a smell of dust, too, at Miss Hubbard's cottage. She had put her carpet on the washing-line, and she was giving it a good beating.

"Just getting the cobwebs out," she said. "You must be Jim. I heard you were coming round with Pat. Would you like to join the church choir?"

"Well, I'll only be here for a week, while Pat's on holiday," said Jim.

"Oh, that's all right," said Miss Hubbard. "You can easily pop over from Pencaster for services. Do you sing bass? We need a good bass."

"Well, er . . ."

"Yes, I should think you do. I'll just put your name down, and we'll see you at the practice on Thursday at seven; now you won't be late, will you?"

"Well, er . . . no . . . I'll not be late."

"Now, Pat, the sun's very strong in Sussex, and you'll need a good pair of sunglasses. I bought these in the jumble-sale last Saturday. They don't fit me, but they'll be just the thing for you. Try them now."

Pat perched the sunglasses on his nose. He did look funny!

"Thank you very much, Miss Hubbard. I'll be glad of these in the Sussex sun. Goodbye!"

"Bye, Pat, and have a good holiday."

As Pat and Jim drove away, they could hear the thump thump of Miss Hubbard beating the dust out of her carpet.

"I had no idea I was going to join a choir," said Jim.

"You'll have to watch out with Miss Hubbard," said Pat, laughing. "She's a right one for roping people in."

Pat and Jim sat down by the lake to eat their sandwiches.

"This is really grand," said Jim. "I don't know why you want a holiday."

When they called at the village school, everyone waas busy with the school bookshop.

"Would you like a book to read on the train?" said Katy.

"Mmmm . . . that sounds like a good idea," said Pat. "What have you got?"

"This looks good," said Katy. "'The Hobbit'. It's about dragons and magic."

"Yes," said Pat. "Thanks. It'll make a change from parcels and letters. I'll try that. Have you any books about singing, for Jim?"

But they couldn't find one, so Pat and Jim went on their way.

Granny Dryden thought she had the wrong glasses on, when she saw Jim at the door.

"I thought you looked different," she said, when she spotted Pat at last, after three changes of glasses. "It must be the holidays."

"It is," said Pat, and told her about Brighton.

"I was there in 1920," said Granny Dryden, "after the war. I have a book about it. It has a map in it, too. You'll have to take it. Now, let's see, where did I put it?"

She changed her glasses twice, and opened the big old bookcase. There was a funny dusty smell, and soon she found the guide to Brighton. It was dated 1911!

"Don't you think it might be a bit out of date?" said Pat.

"Oh, no, things don't change all that much. You'll see," said Granny Dryden. "Anyway, the old times were the best times. Take it, and have a good time."

"Thank you . . . thank you very much," said Pat. "Bye!"

By the time Pat and Jim had finished their round, Pat's van was full of things for his holiday.

"It's not like this in Pencaster," said Jim.

"Well, I hope you enjoy doing the Greendale run," said Pat.

"I'm sure I will," said Jim. "But there's something I must not forget. I have a present, too, for you take on holiday."

"Oh?" said Pat. "What can it be?"

It was a pen and a book of stamps. "Just to remind you to send us some cards," said Jim, "from Brighton."

"It'll make a change to write them, instead of delivering them," said Pat. "Come on, Jess, we'd better go and pack. Cheerio!"

"Cheerio!" said Jim. "And have a good time."

Postman Pat
at the Seaside

At last the day had come for Pat's holiday to begin. Pat woke early, feeling funny inside; how strange it would be, not to be delivering any letters for a whole week! He woke his wife, Sara, and Sara woke young Julian. He looked to see where Jess was, then remembered that Jess had gone to stay with Mrs. Pottage. When they looked outside; it was raining.

"Never mind," said Pat. "We'll have a good time, whatever it does."

There was no time to worry about the weather. They had to catch the first bus to Pencaster, and then catch the train to Brighton. What a rush! They were eating breakfast, packing, and making sandwiches for the train, all at once. Julian went to stand by the gate, in his new raincoat, and under Pat's big umbrella. He was watching for the first sight of the bus coming down the valley. He saw a red post-office van go by, and gave a wave.

"There goes Jim with the letters!" he called.

Then he saw the blur of the Pencaster bus, between the trees, as it came over the hill by Thompson Ground. It would be here in ten minutes.

"Quick!" he called, urgently. "The bus's coming!"

Out came Pat and Sara, with the cases. Pat locked the door, and rushed down the garden path. They were ready just in time. There was a grinding of gears as the bus came up the hill, and round the corner, and there it was, swinging its doors open with a hiss. They all tumbled in, and off they went. People waved as they went by. "Bye, Pat, have a good holiday!"

They were soon at Pencaster station. How exciting it was, when the big Inter-City train came rumbling down the line from Carlisle. They felt that their holiday had really begun.

It was a long journey to Brighton. They had sandwiches and a flask of tea, and a big table all to themselves. Sara read a book. Julian and Pat played games, and did puzzles. Quite often, Julian asked, "Are we nearly there, yet?"

And, each time, Pat said, "Not yet . . . we'll have to be patient."

When their legs got stiff, they had a walk to the toilet, or along to the refreshment-place to buy a bag of crisps. They all had a sleep, then another meal; and still they were not there. Just when Julian thought they would never arrive, Pat said, "I think we're nearly there. Come on, tidy up!"

Then they were drawing into Brighton station, with a squeal of brakes. They walked out into a busy street full of people in holiday clothes, and cars and taxis rushing by, and lovely sunshine.

"I wonder if it's still raining in Greendale," said Pat.

They found their boarding house, right by the sea. There was a big pot of tea and a plate of ham sandwiches waiting for them. They did enjoy them. After that, they had a good wash, and unpacked their bags.

The next day, they got up early, and went on the beach. Ted Glen's rucksack came in handy for carrying all their things. Julian built a large sandcastle with Katy and Tom's bucket and spade. Pat took a picture of him with Mrs. Pottage's camera. Sara wore Miss Hubbard's sun-glasses to read her book, whilst she sunbathed.

"What about a swim?" said Sara.

Pat put on Alf Thompson's striped bathing costume, and the water-wings.

"You do look funny," said Sara.

"Never mind," said Pat. "They'll keep me afloat."

They did, too. Sara and Julian had new costumes, and they splashed and played in the water with Pat. They had a lovely time, and when bedtime came at last, they were all tired, and happy, and sunburnt.

The next day, Pat found Granny Dryden's old guide to Brighton in his case.

"Let's have a look at this," he said. "It might give us some ideas for things to do."

There was a picture of a little electric railway, running along the beach.

"Can we go on that, please?" said Julian.

"We can if it's still there," said Pat. "It is a very old guide."

They went to look, following the map in the guide. It *was* there, with a new coat of paint, and full of people. So they joined the queue, and Pat bought tickets to the end of the line.

"Where does it go?" said Julian.

"Granny Dryden's book says it goes to a little village called Rottingdean," said Pat.

They rumbled along the beach in the little open-air carriage, to the end of the line. But they were not at Rottingdean when they got out. They could see where the lines had once been, running out over the rocks, where children were dabbling in pools for crabs.

"Goodness," said Sara, "it must have been under the water when the tide was in."

"So it was," said Pat. "There's a picture of it, here, with the train on long legs to keep it out of the water!"

Pat asked the man at the ticket-kiosk, and he laughed, and said, "That was a long time ago, a very long time!"

There was so much to do in Brighton, that the week went by very quickly. They went on the little railway another day, and walked out on the rocks, to play in the pools, watching the crabs and the anemones.

They went on the round-abouts and the big-dipper at the fair. They went to see the dolphins, and on the pier. They had a ride on an open-topped bus. They went on the sea in a fast speed-boat. The week was almost over, when Sara said, "We haven't sent any cards!"

"Oh, dear," said Pat, "we must send cards to our friends at home."

He found Jim's pen and book of stamps; they counted up all the cards they had to send, and sat on the beach, writing things like, "Wish you were here," or "Having a lovely time," or "Greetings from sunny Brighton!"

"We'd better get these posted right now," said Pat, "or I'll have to deliver them myself, next week."

The week came to an end, and it was time to pack up and go home. Sara and Julian were sad to be leaving, but Pat said, "I'll be glad to get home. I'm missing the mountains: but we'll come again, next year."

Pat was back on his round on Monday morning. He returned all the things he had borrowed for his holiday, and everyone thanked him for his cards. It was nice to see the pictures of Brighton on the sideboards and mantelpieces of Greendale. All his friends wanted to hear the full story of Pat's week in Brighton, so he was late home that day.

As for Jess, he had had a fine time at Mrs. Pottage's, lapping creamy milk and chasing mice, and he didn't tell anyone anything about it, at all.

Pat Takes Off!

Pat's holiday was over, but it was still summer in Greendale. Some days were hot and sunny; some days it poured with rain. People came to Greendale for their holiday. They walked over the hills, and pitched their tents in Alf Thompson's fields. Pat brought the campers letters from their friends in the town, and collected their postcards with pictures of the mountains and lakes on them, to send to their friends in the towns.

Everyone looked forward to seeing Pat's van. There were other vans, too, that came along the valley. The milk-van came very early, whilst Pat was still in bed. Then there was Sam Waldron, with his mobile shop; the butcher's van came on Wednesdays, and the fish-man on Thursdays. The Pencaster bus came by twice a day. The one that young Julian liked best of all was the mobile-library. This had two people on it – Jack, the driver, and Nellie, the library-lady. They stopped by the garden gate, opened the sliding door, and let down a little step. Then Jack would give a toot on his horn, to tell you they were there. When you went inside, all the walls were covered with books, just

like a real library. Nellie had bright blue eyes. She helped you to find your books, then stamped the date in them in purple ink. Jack told stories about all the people he knew in Greendale and Pencaster. Sara was so busy listening to Jack, that she almost forgot to pick her books. She used to say, "Jack's stories are better than the ones in the books."

Julian never forgot to pick his books. He went straight to the shelf of picture-books at the back of the van. One day, he found a book called, "The Flying Postman". It had lovely pictures, and it was a story about a postman who flew in a small aeroplane to deliver his letters. When Pat came home for his tea, Julian showed him the book. They sat in the big armchair, and Pat read the story to Julian.

"Hmm," said Pat, "what do you think of that? A flying postman! Goodness me, I could get round quickly with an aeroplane. I could whizz over the hills in a twinkling, and drop the letters down the chimney-pots."

"They'd get sooty, and burn up in the fire," said Julian.

"I'll not bother, then," said Pat.

"Tea's ready!" Sara called.

The next day, there was a letter for Pat, from the post-office in Brighton. It was rather a strange letter. It began:

"Dear Pat, How would you like to meet Prince Charles?"

"Prince Charles?" said Pat. "Whatever is all this about?"

He found out when he read the rest of the letter. The Post Office was having a big celebration, for its 350th birthday.

"I didn't know it was as old as that," said Pat, "though it feels like it sometimes."

"You are invited to the celebrations, at Bagshot Park, on 30th July," the letter went on. "Prince Charles will fly in by helicopter, and there will be many exhibitions and displays."

"Can we all go?" said Julian.

"Of course," said Pat. "But where is it? I'll ask Miss Hubbard to look in her atlas."

Pat thought about the invitation all day, and he told all his friends that he was going to meet Prince Charles himself. When he called on Miss Hubbard, she got the big atlas down from its shelf, and looked up Bagshot.

"Bless us!" she said. "It's a long way away from Greendale. You'll have to get a train to London, and then another train to Bagshot. You'll nearly be back at Brighton!"

"Oh dear," said Pat, "I've used up all my holiday for this year. Julian and Sara will be sad if we can't go."

But another letter came by the next post, from the Head Postmaster in Pencaster. He said it was a great honour for Pat to be invited to Bagshot, and that he could have time off to go. With the letter, there was a free railway-ticket for the journey, for Pat, Sara, and Julian. They all shouted, "Hurrah!"

"It will be like an extra holiday," said Pat.

And so it was. They set out again, one sunny morning, on the bus and the train, for Bagshot. This time, they also had a taxi ride across London, in a big black London taxi. Then there was another train to catch, and at last they arrived at Bagshot.

That was a surprise, too, because it was a tiny country station. When the train had rumbled away, there was no one about at all. There was an empty platform, a road going off into the trees, and no sign of the celebrations.

"Where is everyone?" said Pat. "I suppose we'd better walk down this road." They came to a main road, with cars whizzing along. There was a small town, with a few shops.

"It's not as big as Pencaster," said Sara.

Then they spotted a big gate, with a policeman standing by it.

"That looks like a park," said Julian.

"We'll ask that policeman," said Pat, "he looks nice and helpful."

Pat showed the policeman his ticket for the celebrations, and the policeman said, "This way, sir," and they were soon walking up a long drive, lined by trees, with fields full of cows on each side. "It's like Greendale, only flatter," said Pat.

Then a helicopter zoomed overhead, just above the trees. "It's not like Greendale," said Pat.

It was a long walk up the drive. At first, they could only see trees and little rounded hills. Then they saw tents, post-office vans and trucks, and lots of policemen.

"There it is," said Julian, hopping with excitement. "Hurry up!"

It was a lovely show, and there were hundreds of postmen and their families, there to enjoy the fun.

"I didn't know there were so many postmen," said Pat.

There was a display of old post-office vans and uniforms.

"I wouldn't like to wear that one," said Pat, "and I'd get on badly riding a horse!"

"What's that big thing over there?" said Julian.

They went to see. It was a hot-air balloon. It puffed up into the air when the fire roared into its mouth, and swelled and billowed until it was the biggest thing they had ever seen. There was a large basket fastened underneath it, hanging from ropes. A postman came up to them, and said, "Would you like to ride?"

"Oooooh, yes please," said Julian, before Pat had a chance to speak. The postman led them across the grass, and lifted Julian into the basket. Pat climbed in after him, and held on to the rope with all his strength. He felt a bit wobbly at the knees.

"I'll stay on the ground, thanks," said Sara.

The man made the fire roar into the balloon, and, slowly, the basket lifted off the ground.

"Oh, dear," said Pat, "I'm not sure that I want to be a flying postman, after all."

They rose up and up, above the tree-tops. Julian looked down, and saw the people below, looking up at them, growing smaller and smaller. He waved to Sara. Pat didn't dare to look down. He closed his eyes tightly. "I hope we're soon going down." he said.

"It's great!" cried Julian. "I want to go up into the clouds."

They rose still higher, way above the trees, now, until they could see far across the hills of Surrey. The balloon was tied to the ground by a long rope, so that it would not drift right away. Now they were at the end of the rope, and they could feel it pulling at them. The man turned the fire off, and the ballon began to sink down again. Down past the tree-tops, until they touched the ground with a gentle

bump.

"That was *lovely*," said Julian. "Thank you very much. I think I'll be a flying-postman when I grow up."

"Thank you," said Pat. "Oh dear, I do feel funny. It's lovely to be on the ground again."

He walked in a wobbly way, back to Sara. Julian stayed in the basket and went up again with the next lot of people.

There was more flying later on, with a man in a tiny aeroplane.

"That's like the plane in that book," said Julian.

"It's a microlite," said Pat, "and I'm not going up in it."

It swooped and zoomed over and round the trees, looping back and forth, like a swallow. "I'd love to go in it," said Julian.

But it had only one seat for the pilot.

"You've done enough flying for one day," said Sara.

"I've done enough for ever," said Pat.

The next excitement began with a big RAF helicopter coming in low over the trees. A crackly voice on the loudspeakers told them that this was Prince Charles arriving with the new stamps that had been made specially for the day. The helicopter landed by a big house, some distance away amongst the trees. There was quite a long wait, whilst the prince met all the important people.

Then there was the sound of a trumpet, and a clatter of horses' hooves, and Prince Charles rode into the show-ring sitting high up on an old-fashioned stage-coach, next to the coachman. There was a cheer from the crowd, and music playing on the speakers. Pat held Julian up, so that he could see.

The Prince chatted with some postmen in old-fashioned uniforms, and made a speech. There was short play about how King Charles the First started the post all those years ago. There were more speeches. The Prince went to see the exhibitions, and soon it was time for him to fly home in the big helicopter.

"I'm glad I didn't have to meet him," said Pat. "I wouldn't have known what to say."

"You could have told him about your ride in the balloon," said Sara.

They had a picnic under the trees, and saw more of the show.

After a long and busy day, it was time, at last, to catch the train home. Julian was so tired that he slept nearly all the way. It was dark, and late, when they arrived at Pencaster station. The Reverend Timms had come to meet them in the old car they knew so well. They were so glad to see him.

"And how did you get on, at Bagshot?" he said.

But they were all too tired to tell him.

"We'll tell you properly tomorrow," said Pat.

How dark and quiet Greendale seemed, after all the rush and busyness of the day, as the Reverend Timms drove along the winding roads. Owls called in the shadow of the elms, and bats flitted through the headlights. A fox barked somewhere on the hillside. The moon shone on the lake.

"It's good to be back," said Pat.

The Floating Postman

It had rained without stopping for a whole week. On Monday morning it was still raining.

"I don't think much of this for summer weather," grumbled Pat. "I'll have to wear my wellies today."

Jess liked it even less. He curled his tail tightly round himself, as he looked out at the sopping garden.

Rain or no rain, the letters had to be delivered. Pat set out in his little red van. All along the valley, the streams were full of water as they fell down the sides of the hills. They made white lines, as the water churned and foamed.

It looks bad," said Pat to Jess. "Really bad."

When they called at the village post-office, Mrs. Goggins said, "We'll be having floods if this goes on. Just mind how you go, Pat. We don't want you being washed away. I remember last time we had floods; there's a mark on the church wall to show where the water came to. Miss Hubbard was cut off for a week that time."

There was a letter for the Reverend Timms, and Pat asked the Reverend to show him the mark, when he called.

"Goodness," said Pat, "that would come up to my waist, and I'm not much good at swimming."

"The Lord will preserve us," said the Reverend.

Further along the road, Pat saw Peter Fogg, and stopped to give him a letter from his girl-friend in Pencaster. Peter was mending the wall, just by the place where a stream goes under the road.

"Just look at this wall," said Peter. "That water's knocked it down during the night. It's amazing what it can do."

"Watch it doesn't wash you away as well," said Pat.

"Oh, I'll be all right," said Peter. "I'm used to it."

Pat went on his way. At Greendale Farm Mrs. Pottage was grumbling about the weather, too.

"We'd got nearly all the hay in when it started," she said. "There was just one more field to cut, and that's ruined, now."

"Well, it could be worse," said Pat. "You could have lost the lot."

Katy and Tom were not bothering about the weather. They were playing with the farm kittens in the barn, and making houses with bales of hay.

Off Pat went, along the winding roads. Then; "Hold tight, Jess!" he shouted, and stood on the brakes.

Round a corner, the road came to an end! It looked like the beach at Brighton, with the tide coming in. The water lapped right across the road, and three ducks were swimming and dabbling in it.

"What a mess," said Pat. "Now what are we going to do?"

He got out of his van, and stood at the edge of the water. The flood stretched along the road as far as he could see. The river had burst over its banks, and flooded the whole of that part of the valley.

Jess stayed in the van, where it was warm and dry.

"I wonder if Ted Glen ever got round to mending Mr. Pottage's boat," said Pat. "We might be able to get to his place, if we go back a bit. It's worth trying."

So Pat turned his van round, and went to see Ted Glen.

When Pat stopped at Ted Glen's workshop, he could hear a sound of hammering. "It sounds as though he's busy with it, now," said Pat.

He knocked, and walked in. Ted had pulled the boat in through the barn doors (his workshop had once been a barn) and turned the rowing-boat upside down. He had put a new piece of wood in, to replace a rotten piece, and given it a new coat of paint. Now he was putting a new seat in it.

"Hello," said Pat, "I'm glad to see you're getting on with the boat, at last."

"I thought I'd better," said Ted. "If it rains much longer, I'll be able to row it back to Mr. Pottage, and that lake's getting too close for comfort."

"Is that new paint dry?" said Pat.

"Of course it is," said Ted.

"Well I have news for you." said Pat. "The valley road's flooded, and I can't get any further. If we could get this boat afloat, we could get to all the people who must be cut off, and get all these letters through as well."

"We can put it on the trailer, and tow it down to the water with your van," said Ted. "Are you feeling strong? Get hold of that side, and lift when I say go."

The boat was heavy. They rolled it over somehow, and lifted it on to the trailer. Once it was on wheels, it was easy to move. They hitched it to Pat's van, and off they went, with the boat bouncing along the road behind them. Jess looked out at the boat, wondering what on earth it was.

When they reached the edge of the flood, Pat saw that the water had risen still higher whilst he had been at Ted's. He backed the trailer up to the edge of the water. Then they pushed the trailer into the water, until it was deep enough for the boat to float. Ted loosened the ropes, and they felt the water lifting the boat.

"It's stronger than us," said Ted.

"It's like a hot-air balloon," said Pat. "You can feel it lifting away, just the same, only it's wet."

"We'd better take Jess with us," said Ted. "We can't leave him in the van, in case it gets washed away."

Pat went to get Jess. Jess did not want to go in the boat, and dug his claws into Pat's sleeve.

"Come on, Jess, you'll have to come with us," said Pat. "You'll be all right. I'll look after you."

He tucked Jess into his warm coat. His black and white face looked out at the water, and he twitched his whiskers and sneezed, but he felt warm and safe with Pat.

Pat and Ted rowed along the flooded road.

"We'd better go to Miss Hubbard's first," said Ted, "she was cut off for weeks last time we had a flood."

They could see Miss Hubbard's cottage, on its little knoll, from a long way away. The water had flooded all round it, and left it standing on a tiny island. Miss Hubbard was in the garden, in her wellingtons and her bright yellow raincoat and rainhat, looking out for them. They rowed up to her island, and Ted tied the boat up to the gate-post.

"Thank goodness you've come," said Miss Hubbard. "I am glad to see you, I can tell you. There's a special choir-practice at Pencaster church, at two o'clock, and I mustn't miss it."

"Oh, Miss Hubbard, you and your choir-practices!" said Ted. "The whole valley's flooded. You'll not be able to get to Pencaster."

"Nonsense!" said Miss Hubbard. "The telephone's still working, and I've had a word with Reverend Timms. The road to the vicarage is still dry, and he's offered to drive me to Pencaster. He's invited to tea with the bishop. He can't miss that."

That wasn't all. She insisted on bringing her bike as well. How it made the boat rock, when they put the bike in it! They all squeezed in, and Miss Hubbard helped Pat to row, whilst Ted held on to her bike. They rowed across the flood, back to Pat's van.

"I nearly forgot," said Pat. "There are three letters for you, Miss Hubbard."

"Lovely," she said, "I'll read them on the way to Pencaster."

Then she wobbled off along the road, on her bike.

"I hope she gets there," said Ted.

"Now," said Pat, "I wonder if we can get to George Lancaster's place? There's a parcel here for him, from the vet. It's for that sheepdog of his; it's been very poorly. He'll be needing that really urgently."

"We can row across the lake," said Ted. "Then you can walk up the hill to George's. It'll be a long wet walk, but it's the only way."

"Right-o," said Pat. "Let's be on the way. Thanks for helping, Ted."

They rowed across the lake, to the nearest point to the road to Intake Farm. They were in luck, because George had driven down on his tractor, to see if there was a way through the water. He had driven his tractor into the water, but it became so deep that he had to turn back. He was just on his way home, when he saw Pat and Ted.

Pat shouted, "Hi! George! We've brought your parcel from the vet."

George stopped his tractor and waited for them to come close.

"By Jove, I am glad to see you," he said. "My poor old Bess is in a real bad way. That's her medicine. It'll put her on her feet in no time."

"I thought it looked important," said Pat.

"You haven't got a box of matches as well, have you?" said George. "I'm down to my last three matches."

"You're in luck," said Ted. "I have some. Catch!"

"Are you all right for food?" said Pat.

"Yes, we always keep a good store of tins. We'll be OK. Thanks, Pat and Ted. I'll see you when this water gets away. Cheerio!"

Off he went, up the hill, on his tractor. Ted and Pat rowed back across the lake. On the way, they saw a goat standing on the roof of a hen-hut, trapped by the flood.

"Poor thing," said Pat, "we'd better see if we can get it into the boat."

What a struggle they had with that goat. It did not want to go in the boat.

It kicked, and butted, and struggled; and it was strong. It was a wonder they didn't all fall in the water, but they got it in somehow. Ted had to tie its legs with a piece of rope, to stop it jumping out again.

"I'll have to ask Mrs. Pottage to put it in a spare pen, until the floods go down," said Pat. "It's sure to try to run home, if it's in a field."

Jess was very cross when they put the goat in Pat's van. He hated sharing his van with a goat, even if its legs were tied together. The goat glared at him in a very fierce way all the way to Greendale Farm. As soon as she saw the goat, Mrs. Pottage said, "That's Poppy; she's one of Alf Thompson's goats. She's a real devil; always breaking out, and jumping over fences and walls. She had no business being down where the floods are. It serves her right! She can stay in our spare pig-sty, until she can go home, and she'd better behave herself."

They carried Poppy to the pig-sty, and untied her legs. She jumped and frisked about, and butted the wooden door, but she could not get out.

"Be a good girl, and you can have some dinner," said Mrs. Pottage.

"We've brought your boat, as well," said Ted. "Thanks for lending it, though you didn't know you were."

"That's all right," said Mrs. Pottage. "You're welcome. We'd better keep it ready, in case it's needed tomorrow to rescue anyone."

Pat drove Ted home.

"I think the water's dropping," said Pat, as they looked over the wall at the flood.

"And look," said Ted, "the sun's coming out."

It was, too. The clouds rolled away, and there was a big stretch of blue sky. The sun shone, and began to dry up the water.

"I hope it's better tomorrow," said Pat. "I'd rather keep my feet dry. Thanks for all your help, Ted. Cheerio!"

Pat and Jess were on their way home, looking forward to their tea, to dry clothes and dry paws.

The next morning, the floods had gone down so much that the roads were mostly clear. There was a lot of mud and rubbish everywhere, and some deep puddles, but Pat could get through in his van, with a deal of spattering and splashing.

Alf came to take Poppy home, and give her a good telling off for wandering, just as she was looking forward to a second bucket of Mrs. Pottage's mash.

Miss Hubbard stayed overnight in Pencaster; the vicar's wife put her in the best spare room. She did some shopping in town, and came home on the Greendale bus, to find that the flood had washed her garden gate away, but nothing worse.

"That's another job for Ted," she said. "I'll pop round in the morning. I think I'll have a blue one, this time."

A Wild
Pig Chase

One Friday afternoon, Pat opened the door, said, "Good heavens!" and closed the door with a bang.

"What's wrong?" said Sara.

"There's a pig in the garden," said Pat, "and it's eating our cabbages."

"A pig? Did you say a pig?" said Sara. "We'd better get it out, before it eats the strawberries. Quick, get your shoes on!"

Julian and Jess came to see what was going on, and they all ran out into the garden. As soon as Jess saw the pig, he ran up the apple tree, and climbed up and up, until he was in the very top. The fat little pig was snuffling about in the lettuces, now.

"It looks like one of Alf Thompson's," said Pat.

"Never mind whose it is, let's chase it out of our garden," said Sara. "It's going to get those strawberries."

Pat opened the gate. They all began to shout and shoo at the pig; but it liked their garden, and it took no notice at all. It just went on munching a nice crisp lettuce.

"I was going to make a salad with that lettuce," said Sara, getting cross. "It's the best one."

The pig headed towards the strawberries. "It's not having my lovely
strawberries," said Sara.

She picked up a stick, and gave the
pig a whack. Now the pig was cross. It
snorted, kicked up its heels, and ran
straight through a flower-bed. It ran all
over the garden. Sara, and Pat, and
Julian, ran after it. They dodged, and
shouted; they waved sticks, and banged
buckets; but they could not catch it. It
never went near the open gate. It knocked a
bucket into a cold-frame and smashed all
the glass. It bumped into the clothes-prop, and
dropped the clean washing in the dirt. It crushed
the flowers, and trampled through the strawberries.
It squealed and snorted. Jess sat in the top of the tree,
with all his claws out, and stared down at them all. At
last, the pig pushed through the hedge, and out into the
road. Pat banged the gate shut.

"It's no good leaving it there," said Sara. "It's made a hole in the hedge, now. It can get back in, easily."

"And it can't stay in the road," said Pat, "it'll get run over. I'd better chase it back home."

The pig was trotting off down the road at a good speed. Pat jumped on his bike and rode after it. Sara and Julian went to pick the strawberries, and finish their tea. Jess stayed in the tree.

Pat rode along the road to the village, with the pig trotting ahead of him. It tried to get into the school garden, but Pat headed it off, and it went on towards the post-office. The door was open, and in went the pig. Pat heard something fall over, then Mrs. Goggins shouting. A lot of potatoes rolled across the floor, and the pig ran out with a big potato in its mouth, with Mrs. Goggins after it. Pat tried to stop it with his bike, but it was too quick for him, and it was off down the village street, with its hooves going clickety-click on the cobbles. Katy and Tom came out of the sweet-shop with ice-lollies in their hands. The pig dropped its potato. Then it chased Katy round the old water-pump, until she dropped her lolly; it gobbled it up, stick and all. Katy began to cry.

Pat came and gave her some money to get another lolly. Off went the pig. Off went Pat, after it.

The pig ran in at the churchyard gate. Pat left his bike by the wall, and ran after it. The pig seemed to think they were playing a game. It dodged Pat all round the churchyard.

It hid behind gravestones, then jumped out and ran off, just as Pat came up to it. He chased the pig four times round the church. He was getting puffed, but the pig never seemed to get tired. Pat sat down in the porch to get his breath back. He could hear the sound of the organ.

"Hm," said Pat, "that must be Miss Hubbard practising for the service on Sunday. What a nice, peaceful, sound it is. I wonder if she knows how to catch a pig?"

Then Pat heard voices. Someone was walking round the churchyard.

"That sounds like the Reverend Timms and Dr. Gilbertson. I expect they've come for the choir-practice," said Pat.

Pat heard another sound. A strange ripping and tearing sound. He stood up, and looked out of the church porch.

"Oh, no!"

A large bunch of flowers, and a pile of new hymn-books, had been left on the seat by the gate. The pig had eaten most of the flowers, and now it was tearing up the hymn-books! Pat ran down the path, shouting at it. The Reverend Timms and Dr. Gilbertson, at the far side of the churchyard, looked round to see what was happening. Then they came running, and off went the pig again, to hide behind the gravestones. What a mess it had made!

"Bless us, and save us," said the Reverend Timms, "whatever has happened?"

Pat told them the whole story of the pig, and all the trouble it had made.

"It is one of God's creatures," said the Reverend Timms, "and we must try to forgive it."

"The silly creature," said Dr. Gilbertson; "it doesn't know how naughty it is, I don't suppose."

"Of course she does!" said another voice. It was Miss Hubbard. She had left off practising the organ, to come and see what was going on. "That is the naughtiest creature I ever knew," she said. "I told Alf to take her to market, two months ago. He's had nothing but trouble with her, but I reckon he has a soft spot for her, all the same. Anyway, it's no good standing here, while she plans more mischief."

"Well I hope you know how to catch her," said Pat. "She's beaten me."

Miss Hubbard smiled, and said, "Oh, no, you can't catch her. We'll have to send for Alf. Now, Reverend, I suggest that you pop back to the vicarage, and ring Alf. He'll bring his Landrover, a few nice carrots, and a large sack, and all will be well."

The Reverend Timms did just as Miss Hubbard had said. Alf came at once. He waved the carrots at the pig, and called to her, "Come on, Maggy, nice carrots, lovely carrots. Come on, girl."

While the pig was busy munching the carrots, he popped the sack over her head. Then he carried the wriggling, squealing, bundle to the Landrover, put it in the back, and closed the door firmly.

Alf said how sorry he was for all the trouble Maggy had made, and insisted on paying for everything.

Then the Reverend Timms said, "I think we all need some refreshment after all this excitement." So they all went to the vicarage, and had tea and cakes.

When Pat cycled home, later on, Sara and Julian had saved some strawberries and cream for him. He told them all about his adventures with the pig. Then Sara said, "Now you'd better get the ladder out."

"Why?" said Pat.

"Because," said Sara, "Jess is still up that tree, and he can't get down."